George Catches a Cold

Published by arrangement with Entertainment One and Ladybird Books, A Penguin Company.
This book is based on the TV series Peppa Pig. Peppa Pig is created by Neville Astley and Mark Baker.
Peppa Pig © Astley Baker Davies Ltd/Entertainment One UK Ltd 2003.

ISBN 978-1-338-05419-4

10 9 8 7 6 5 4 3 2 1
Printed in the U.S.A.

17 18 19 20 21
40

First printing 2017
Book design by Angela Jun

www.peppapig.com

SCHOLASTIC INC.

Mummy Pig says Peppa and George can play in the rain, but they must wear rain clothes to keep dry.

But George hates wearing his rain hat,
so he has thrown it in a muddy puddle.
Peppa knows that is not a good idea.

Hee, hee!

"Come inside, children," calls Daddy Pig. "It's raining too hard now."

"Where's your hat, George?" asks Mummy Pig.

"Atchoo!" replies George.

Oh, dear. George has caught a cold.

"AAAATCHOOOOO!"

George cannot stop sneezing.
"Poor little George," says
Mummy Pig. "You don't look very well."
"Don't worry. I'll call Doctor Brown Bear,"
says Daddy Pig.

"Will George go to the hospital?" asks Peppa.
"No, George has to go to bed," replies Daddy.
"So George is not truly sick then,"
says Peppa, disappointed.

"George, you have to
stay in bed until you are
better," says Daddy Pig.
"Why?" asks George.
"Because you have to
keep warm," says Daddy.

Doctor Brown Bear is here to see George. "Open wide and say ahhhh," he says. George is a little afraid of Doctor Brown Bear. He hides under his sheets with Mr. Dinosaur.

Doctor Brown Bear asks Peppa to show George that he does not have to be scared.

"Ahhhh," says Peppa.

George laughs and comes out from under his sheets. He opens his mouth so Doctor Brown Bear can look.

"Ahhh," says George.

"George has caught a cold," Doctor Brown Bear
tells Mummy Pig. "He can have some warm milk at
bedtime to help him sleep."
"Thank you, Doctor Brown Bear!" says Mummy Pig.

"You're welcome. Good-bye!" says Doctor Brown Bear, before driving off in his special white car.

The next morning, George wakes up early.
The warm milk made him sleep very well.
"Roar!" cries George, waking up Peppa. He is
feeling much better.

Roar!

Hee, hee, hee!

It's a lovely sunny day but George is wearing his rain hat. He doesn't want to catch another cold.

"Oh, George! You don't need to wear your hat when it is warm and sunny!" Mummy Pig tells him.

"Hee, hee, hee!" everyone laughs.

George never goes in the rain
without his hat again.